Me and My Grandad

Alison Ritchie • Alison Edgson

LiTTLE TiGER

LONDON

My grandad is here,
it's my BEST kind of day!
I hop on his back
and we're up and away.

As we skip through the woods,
there's SO much to see.
We call out the names
of each flower and tree.

We whizz down the hillside
and land with a thud.
Grandad looks funny
all covered in mud!

It's time for a wash,
so we jump in the lake.
Grandad's BIG splash
makes the whole woodland shake!

When we play hide-and-seek,
I climb right up the tree.
Grandad is clever
but never finds me!

With his bright, beaming smile
and a cheery hello,
My grandad makes friends
wherever we go!

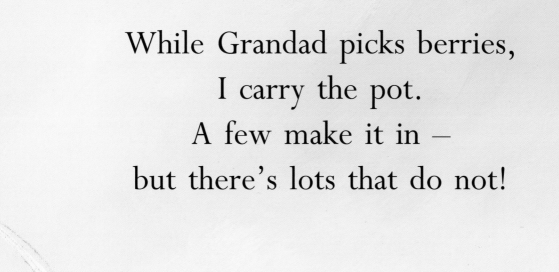

While Grandad picks berries,
I carry the pot.
A few make it in –
but there's lots that do not!

If something is wrong
and I start to feel blue,
My grandad is there
and knows just what to do!

The den we've been building
is finished at last.
I clamber inside it
but Grandad's stuck fast!

As the sun starts to set,
we sing songs by the fire.
Our friends join in too –
we're the marshmallow choir!

When we're cosy back home,
Grandad tucks me up tight.
Then he gives me a hug
and a big kiss goodnight.

Grandad's my hero,
he's funny and smart.
I love my grandad
with ALL of my heart.

More heart-warming stories from Little Tiger…

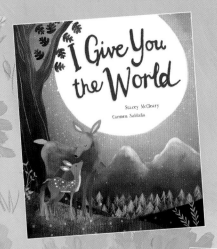

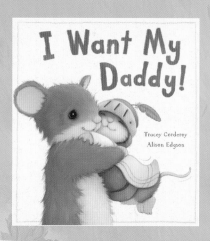

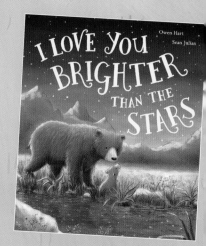

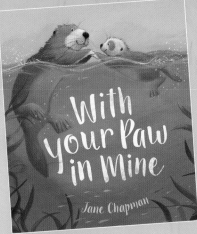

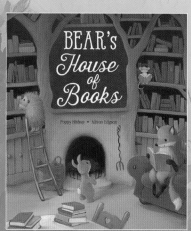

For information regarding any of the above titles or for our catalogue, please contact
Little Tiger Press Ltd, 1 Coda Studios, 189 Munster Road, London SW6 6AW
Tel: 020 7385 6333 • E-mail: contact@littletiger.co.uk • www.littletiger.co.uk